First published in 2001 by Brimax
an imprint of Octopus Publishing Group Ltd
2-4 Heron Quays, London, E14 4JP
© Octopus Publishing Group Ltd
Printed in Spain

CONTENTS

SILLY TILLY WITCH

Tilly Witch had a big hole in her roof.
Whenever it rained, water dripped
through all day and all night.
"Drip! Drip! Drip!" said Tilly. "I am
tired of getting wet."
So she wore her big, black hat to keep
dry. She wore it in the bath. She wore
it in bed. She never, ever took it off.

"I must find my book of spells," said Tilly one day. "Then I can magic a new, dry roof."

Tilly looked under her bed and under the cat. She looked inside her cooking pot and inside her boots. She shook her broomstick and her thick socks. But she could not find her book of spells anywhere.

Tilly climbed onto the roof and
sat down.
"I cannot mend this big hole,"
she said. "I will try to think of
some magic."
She sat very still and said a
magic spell.
"Pink jumping frogs,
a blue spotty mouse.
Please magic a roof
for my little house."
Then she waited for the spell to work.

Suddenly the roof began to rock from side to side. Tilly almost fell off. Then the roof rose into the air and began to fly. It flew faster and faster. Tilly held onto the chimney.

"I think that was the wrong spell!" she said. "Oh, I am a silly witch!"

Seagull and some of her friends flew
by. They were flying home to the sea.
"Our wings are very tired," said
Seagull. "We have been flying for a
long time."
"Then sit on my roof for a rest,"
said Tilly.
They held on tightly as the roof
flew on.

Mr. and Mrs. Squirrel ran to the top of a big hill. They waved at the flying roof.

"Our legs are tired," they said. "We have been running for a long time." They jumped onto the roof and sat down for a rest.

"Hold on tightly!" said Tilly as they flew through the sky.

Then they saw Mrs. Robin. Her five
babies were flying with her. They
were all tired.

"Our wings are so small," said the
baby birds. "We cannot fly very well."

"Then come for a ride on my roof,"
said Tilly. "We can fly very quickly."
There was no more room on the roof
as it flew along.

Kitten was sitting on top of the clock tower. She saw the flying roof go by. "Help!" she said. "I am stuck! I cannot get down!"

Tilly picked up Kitten and tried to put her on the roof. There was no more room!

"Kitten can sit in my pocket," said Tilly. "Now hold on tightly!"

Then the big clock began to chime.
BONG! BONG! BONG! BONG!
"It's four o'clock," said Tilly.
"I must get home soon. My house has
no roof."
"But you're a witch," said Mrs.
Squirrel. "You can magic a new roof."
"I wish I could," said Tilly, "but
I have lost my book of spells."

Suddenly the roof began to wobble.
"The magic has gone," said Tilly.
"We are going to fall off!"
The roof crashed into a big, soft pile
of straw. Everyone fell off. Then the
roof rose into the air and flew out
of sight.
"Oh dear," said Tilly. "Now I have no
roof at all. What am I going to do?"

"We can help," said Mrs. Robin.
All of Tilly's friends took big piles of
straw to Tilly's house. Then the birds
began to weave the straw.
"This is how we make our nests," they
said.
They made a warm, dry roof for
Tilly's house.
"Thank you," said Tilly. "How clever
you are."

Tilly's friends stayed for supper. It was getting dark when they went home. Since Tilly was very tired, she got ready for bed. The new roof had no holes in it.

"I will stay warm and dry all night," said Tilly. "At last I can take off my big, black hat."

Tilly hung her hat on the door. As she brushed her hair, she began to smile. On top of her head was the lost book of spells!

"It was under my hat all the time," said Tilly. "Oh, I am a silly witch." Then she put the book under her pillow and fell fast asleep.

Say these words again.

at	rest
it	rock
on	magic
can	small
ran	spells
sat	wobble
hill	getting

What can you see?

roof

hat

broomstick

cooking pot

book of spells

Spooky the Teapot Ghost

Spooky the ghost lived in a big,
pink teapot in a garden shed.
It was an old, dusty teapot.
It had no lid and a funny spout.
Spooky liked his funny home.
No one knew he lived there.
He could fly around all day and
no one could see him.

But Spooky had no friends.
"No one knows who I am," he said.
"No one can see a ghost."
He went to the park and fed the
ducks. He sat on the swings and slid
down the slide. Then he threw a ball
for a dog. But no one spoke to him.
No one knew he was there.

One day Spooky flew out of his teapot. He flew over the town and over the fields. He sat in a tree in Dapple Wood. It was sports day and all the animals were having fun. "Maybe I can have some fun too," said Spooky. "No one can see me, so I can play some tricks."

The first contest was the running
race. The animals stood in a line.
They waited for the race to begin.
"Ready...Steady...Go!" cried Spooky.
All the animals fell over.
"Who said that?" asked Mouse.
They looked all around them, but
no one could see Spooky in the tree.

Then came the high jump. Mouse
fixed a long pole between two trees.
But Spooky moved the pole. He moved
it far too high and no one could jump
over it.
"Who moved the pole?" asked
Mouse.
They looked up in the trees.
No one could see Spooky.

The sack race was next. But Spooky moved the finishing post into the middle of the stream! All the animals were very wet and very angry. "Someone is playing tricks on us," said Mouse.

But they couldn't see Spooky. He waved goodbye as he flew home to his big, pink teapot.

That night Owl tapped on the
window of the garden shed.
"You played those tricks, Spooky," he
said. "I know it was you."
Spooky peeped out of his teapot.
"I am a ghost," said Spooky. "You
cannot see me."
"I cannot see you in the daytime,"
said Owl. "But since you glow in the
dark, I can see you now."

Owl was very kind. Spooky said he was sorry for playing tricks.

"Then come to Dapple Wood with me," said Owl.

They flew off into the dark sky.

"I have never been out in the dark before," said Spooky. "Look! I really am glowing!"

The streets and fields lit up as Spooky flew by.

The animals in Dapple Wood were wide awake. Spooky and Owl flew down beside them. Spooky saw that the animals looked sad.

"What is the matter?" he asked.

"We cannot leave the wood," said Mole.

"We would get lost in the dark," said Bear.

"So we never have any fun," said Rabbit.

"Come with me," said Spooky.
He led the animals to the
garden shed.
"I have never been out of the wood
before," said Rabbit.
"We cannot get lost," said Mole.
"Spooky is glowing like a torch."
"We will take my teapot back to
Dapple Wood," said Spooky. "Then
we can have some fun."
The animals pushed and pulled the
teapot back to Dapple Wood.

Back in Dapple Wood they pushed the
teapot into the stream.
"All aboard!" said Spooky.
But as the animals climbed onto the
teapot, it began to wobble.
"Help!" called Mole. "I am going to
fall!"
Splash! Mole fell into the stream.
Bear and Rabbit pulled him out.
"Now I am all wet," said Mole.
"Never mind," said Spooky. "Now we
are going to have an adventure!"

They sailed down the stream to the river. Soon they were sailing on the sea. They bobbed up and down on the waves. The big, pink teapot landed on the beach. Spooky and the animals played on the sand and looked for seashells.

"This is such fun!" said Rabbit. They played all night on the beach then the next morning they sailed home.

Spooky had so much fun he decided to stay in Dapple Wood with his new friends. Teddy found a warm dry place for Spooky and his teapot. Spooky slept all day. Every night he stayed awake with his new friends. They had lots of fun sailing in the big, pink teapot.

"It is nice being a ghost after all," said Spooky.

Say these words again.

in	said
no	that
of	never
and	garden
the	animals
was	morning
into	sailing

What can you see?

teapot

seashells

ducks

trunk

shed

Sizzle the Dragon

Sizzle the dragon had a bad cold. His nose was red and he sneezed all day long. He tried to blow fire from his nose, but he could only huff and puff. "You have a cold," said his friends. "You will blow fire when you are better."
Sizzle was very grumpy.

"You can have my blue scarf to keep you warm," said Fox.
"And my red scarf," said Rabbit.
"And my yellow scarf," said Cat.
Bee gave Sizzle some honey. Squirrel gave him some acorn tea. But Sizzle was still a very grumpy dragon.

"We must cheer Sizzle up," said Cat. Every day they told Sizzle funny jokes. Rabbit stood on her head and sang songs. Fox ran after his own tail. Bee flew past upside down. But Sizzle did not smile.

"I have a bad cold," he said. "I feel very grumpy."

Then Squirrel juggled nuts in the air.
He dropped two, and three hit him on
the head. Sizzle still did not smile.
Then Fox wore a silly hat and made a
funny face.
But Sizzle was still grumpy.
His friends went away and left him
on his own.

The next day Sizzle woke up early.
"Do you know what day it is today,
Cat?" asked Sizzle.
"It is Friday," said Cat.
"Do you know what day it is today,
Bee?" asked Sizzle.
"Yes, it is Friday," said Bee.
Sizzle felt very grumpy again.
No one knew it was his birthday.

"Please can I have my blue scarf back?" asked Fox.

"And my red scarf," said Rabbit.

"And my yellow scarf," said Cat.

"I am not better yet," said Sizzle.

But he did not sniff or sneeze at all.

He took off the scarves.

"Now my neck is cold," he said.

Sizzle's friends had a lot of work to do. Sizzle was too grumpy to help. He sat under a tree and watched. Fox collected wood. Rabbit made a big pile of leaves. Cat helped Squirrel to carry some boxes. Bee buzzed by with some twigs. Soon there was a big pile of wood and leaves. The animals stood and looked at their bonfire.

"We cannot light our bonfire," said Squirrel.

"Please light our bonfire, Sizzle," asked Fox.

But Sizzle would not even try.

"I cannot blow fire," he said.

"I still have a cold."

But Sizzle's friends knew he was better. Squirrel took a pepper pot and climbed to the top of a tree. He shook pepper over Sizzle.

"My nose tickles," said Sizzle.

Squirrel shook more pepper onto Sizzle.

"Now my nose really tickles," said Sizzle.

Then Sizzle gave a very big sneeze.

"AAATISHOOO!"

Fire and smoke blew from his nose.

It lit the bonfire.

"Well done, Sizzle," said the animals.

"We knew your cold was better."

But Sizzle was still grumpy.

"It is my birthday," he said.

But no one heard him.

Then Sizzle saw Fox's blue scarf, Rabbit's red scarf and Cat's yellow scarf. They were up in the trees. They had HAPPY BIRTHDAY SIZZLE on them in big letters. "You knew it was my birthday all the time!" said Sizzle.

"We are going to have a party,"
said Bee.
They had hot food cooked on the
bonfire. They danced and played
games until it was late. Sizzle had
lots of fun.
"I will never be grumpy again," he
said. "From now on I will smile all
the time."

Cat had made a birthday cake.
"Now that your cold is better, you
can light the candles," she said.
Sizzle blew fire from his nose and lit
all five candles.
"Happy birthday, dear Sizzle, happy
birthday to you!" sang his friends.
Sizzle smiled. He was a very happy
dragon indeed!

Say these words again.

he	still
my	tree
up	happy
had	dragon
hit	grumpy
yet	sneeze
cold	birthday

What can you see?

hat

bonfire

birthday cake

leaves

scarf

Hippopotamus is the friendliest and kindest hippopotamus you will ever meet. He has a very nice smile. He is very kind. And he loves to play.

But if you see Hippopotamus running towards you, you should run away and hide as fast as you can.

That's what all the other animals do because they know what is going to happen next...

First there is a rumbling noise,
and it grows louder and louder
- rumble, rumble, **rumble**.

Then there is a cloud of dust and it gets bigger, and bigger, and **bigger**.

And inside the cloud of dust is Hippopotamus. He is running faster, and **faster**, and **faster**, because he is so pleased to see you. And he is getting closer, and closer, and **closer**.

And he has a great big smile upon his face.

Then if you haven't run away,
he will jump in the air and land
right on top of you - and give
you a great big hug.
But what will happen to you?
You will be squashed as flat
as a piece of paper in this
book, because Hippopotamus
is so much bigger than you.
And he is very, very **heavy**.

Of course Hippopotamus always said sorry when he walked on a baby monkey's toes, or bumped into the baby zebras and knocked them over. But they still cried and ran home to their mothers saying they didn't want to play with him anymore.

So he had no one to play with, and Hippopotamus was very sad.

Every day Hippopotamus sat by himself at the bottom of a tree with great, big tears rolling down his round cheeks. He didn't know how much it hurt to be squashed because nobody had ever squashed him - until one day he met Elephant.

On this particular day it was very hot and dry.

Hippopotamus was sitting under the tree as usual and since he was very thirsty he went to the pond to get a drink. There he saw Elephant having a swim.

Elephant didn't look very big because he was mostly under the water. Hippopotamus could only see his ears and trunk.

"Hello," said Hippopotamus. "Do you want to play a game with me?"

Elephant couldn't hear him because his ears were full of water.

Hippopotamus spoke louder. "HELLO! DO YOU WANT TO PLAY WITH ME?"

This time Elephant heard him. "Hello," he said. And he swam to the side of the pond and began to climb out.

As Elephant came out of the water, Hippopotamus saw that he was very big.

First there were his head and trunk. Then his huge, round body. And lastly there were four enormous legs, each one the size of a tree trunk. Hippopotamus suddenly felt very small.

"What game do you want to play?" asked Elephant, looking down at Hippopotamus.

"Shall we play catch?" replied Hippopotamus. "I like playing catch."

"Yes," said Elephant.

At first the game was great fun. Hippopotamus and Elephant ran backwards and forwards and round and round as fast as they could. Hippopotamus was very happy that he had someone to play with at last.

But then something happened. Hippopotamus fell over when Elephant was running after him. But Elephant was running so fast he couldn't stop.

Crash! He fell onto Hippopotamus and squashed him flat.

"Ow,ow,ow, please get off, you're hurting me!" cried Hippopotamus.

Elephant rolled over and stood up.

"I'm very sorry," he said. "It was an accident. I didn't mean to hurt you."

Hippopotamus made sure that nothing was broken and then he stood up.

"There, there," said Elephant. "I hope you feel better soon."

Hippopotamus did feel better. But now he knew that being squashed wasn't very nice. He also knew why the other animals wouldn't play with him anymore.

The next day Hippopotamus went to find them.

"Please come out wherever you are," he called. "I'm very sorry that I squashed all of you. I promise not to do it again."

One by one, the animals came out from where they had been hiding.

"Do you really promise?" asked a baby zebra.

"Yes, do you really promise?" asked a baby monkey.

"Yes," said Hippopotamus. "I will never squash you again. Please will you play with me now?"

The animals thought for a moment and then decided that they would play with him. And Hippopotamus didn't squash any of them ever again.

Heavy Hippopotamus

Hippopotamus is smooth and round, with four short legs, one at each corner.
He has a round face, big, brown eyes and a huge smile.
He has a squiggly tail.
Hippopotamus is very bouncy, but don't let him bounce on you unless you want to be as flat as a pancake - because he is VERY, VERY HEAVY.

One morning, Hippopotamus was doing his exercises. He bounced up and down - BOING, BOING, BOING.
Then he jumped up and down - UP DOWN THUD, UP DOWN THUD, UP DOWN THUD.
Then he ran around in circles - BADOOM, BADOOM, BADOOM.
That made him dizzy, and he fell over.

None of the other animals liked it when Hippopotamus did his exercises because it made the ground shake.

In fact it made the ground shake **so much** that the birds fell off the trees, the giraffes' necks wobbled from side to side, the zebras' stripes got mixed up, and it gave the lions headaches!

After his exercises
Hippopotamus liked to have a
long bath.
None of the animals liked this
either. There was only room for
Hippopotamus in the pond.
None of the other animals
could get in at the same time
without being squashed. And
by the time Hippopotamus had
cleaned and scrubbed all his
smelly bits, the water was full of
muddy bubbles.

"Being clean is very important," said Hippopotamus. "If I didn't wash I'd be all muddy and smelly. Nobody would like that."

The other animals agreed. But **they** were muddy and smelly because they couldn't get into the pond to wash. So one day the animals decided they would have to find a way to stop Hippopotamus having his bath.

Late that night Hippopotamus heard lots of banging and sawing. He didn't care what was happening because he was very tired. So he went to sleep and he snored very loudly.

A little way away from where Hippopotamus was sleeping, an elephant put down his hammer. He turned to the monkeys, birds, zebras and giraffes standing next to him. "I think everything is ready now," he said. "I don't think Hippopotamus will want his bath tomorrow."

Very early the next morning,
Hippopotamus woke up.
Right away he started his
exercises. He bounced up and
down - BOING, BOING, BOING.
Then he jumped up and down
- UP DOWN THUD, UP DOWN
THUD, UP DOWN THUD. Then he
ran around in circles
- BADOOM, BADOOM,
BADOOM. That made him dizzy
and he fell over.
"That's better," he said. "Time
for my bath now."

He trotted over to the pond and was just about to jump in when he saw something which made him stop.

Right in the middle of the pond were some enormous teeth in an enormous mouth poking up from under the water.
They were the kind of teeth which could bite a hippopotamus and eat him all up.
They looked like the teeth of a crocodile who was hiding under the water. A crocodile just waiting for a hippopotamus to eat for its breakfast.

"Help!" cried Hippopotamus. "Help! There's a crocodile in the pond and I'm too frightened to go in it!"

The elephant heard Hippopotamus and came down to look.

"You're right," said the elephant. "It looks like a very big crocodile to me. You'd better not have your bath today."

All the animals who had come along to see what the noise was about agreed.

"Oh well," said Hippopotamus. "I don't suppose it will matter if I don't have a bath today. Maybe I could have one tomorrow instead if the crocodile has gone away."

"That's a good idea," said the elephant. "Why don't you go for a walk? There are some nice, juicy leaves to eat just over the hill."

"Yes," said Hippopotamus. "That's a very good idea." And off he went.

The animals waited by the pond until they were sure he had gone. Then one by one they jumped into the pond and started to have their baths. One of the birds flew over to the crocodile and sat on the very end of its mouth.

A baby zebra saw this and asked its mother if the bird was going to be eaten.

"No, my dear," said the mother. "You see, that is not a real crocodile. We made it last night out of bits of wood. We made it to stop Hippopotamus getting in the pond."

"Will you tell him it's not a real one?" asked the baby zebra.

"Perhaps one day. When he's very smelly."

And both zebras jumped in and joined the other animals.

Hippopotamus Climbs a Tree

Hippopotamus was very hungry.

He was lying on the ground beneath a banana tree and his tummy was empty. He listened to it making rumbly noises - bloomp bloomp, bloomp bloomp. Then he listened to it making gurgly noises - gluggle luggle, gluggle luggle.

"All I want is one banana," Hippopotamus sighed. "But they are all at the top of the tree and I am at the very bottom."

He rolled over onto his back and looked at one of the biggest bananas on the tree. "Please fall off," he said to the banana.

But the banana just stayed where it was. It didn't want to fall off.

Hippopotamus got more and more hungry.

Just then a monkey ran past Hippopotamus and jumped up into the tree. He climbed until he reached the very top. Then he picked the biggest banana, opened it up and ate it all in one bite. He dropped the banana skin which landed on Hippopotamus' nose.

"Hey, that's not very nice!" said Hippopotamus. "I can't just eat a banana skin."

But the monkey only laughed at him and ran back home.

Hippopotamus stared at the tree and at the bananas growing at the very top.

"How can I get a banana when they are so high up? I do wish I could climb like a monkey," he sighed.

Then he had an idea. After all, if monkeys could get up trees why shouldn't a hippopotamus too?

He looked carefully at the tree. It was smooth and there weren't any branches to hold onto. The tree was very thin and it swayed backwards and forwards as the wind blew. Hippopotamus thought that if he was very careful and climbed up the tree very slowly, he could get to the top. Then he could eat a banana.

Hippopotamus squeezed his front and back legs tightly around the tree and slowly started to climb. But then a strange thing began to happen. As he climbed up the tree, Hippopotamus saw that it was bending over. And the higher up the tree he climbed, the more it bent.

Even so, he still couldn't reach the bananas.

Higher and higher climbed Hippopotamus. And the higher he climbed up the tree the lower it bent down. Until the bananas were almost on the ground.

"Nearly there," said Hippopotamus as he got closer and closer to the top of the tree.

Soon he was so close to the bananas that he could smell them. His tummy gave an extra big rumble and he reached out to pick one.

But as he did one of the leaves on the tree started to tickle the end of Hippopotamus' nose. Of course, he couldn't let go of the tree to brush the leaf away because then he would fall off. So the leaf kept on tickling and tickling until Hippopotamus gave the most enormous sneeze.
"Atishoo!"

He sneezed again. "ATISHOO!"
And then again even more
loudly. "**ATISHOO!**"
Hippopotamus held on as
tightly as he could to the tree
but it was too smooth and
slippery.
He fell to the ground and
landed on his back.
THUD!

Now the tree no longer had
a great big Hippopotamus on
it. It started to unbend and
stand up straight. Up it went
faster and faster rising like
a kite in a strong wind. At last
it was pointing right back up
into the sky.
And as soon as it did the
bananas flew off the top of
the tree.

But instead of falling down the bananas kept going up.
Up and up they went until they could get no higher.
Then they started to fall back to the ground. Slowly at first - then faster and faster.

Hippopotamus was still lying on his back when he saw the bananas going up into the air. Then he saw them coming back down again. He knew exactly where they were going to land - right on top of his head.

But then he had an idea.

As the bananas fell towards him Hippopotamus opened his mouth as wide as he could.

And one by one the bananas dropped straight into his mouth - plop, plop, plop!

Hippopotamus closed his mouth and ate all the bananas at once. There was a big smile all over his face.

The monkey who had climbed the tree before came back. He climbed up it again. But when he got back there were no bananas left at all.

"Where have they all gone?" cried the monkey. "I"m still hungry!"

Hippopotamus smiled some more and pointed to his fat, round tummy.

"They are all in there," he told the monkey. "You're not the only one who can climb trees you know. Hippos are the best banana trees climbers in the whole, wide world."

THE FORGETFUL SPIDER

Spider is putting on his shoes. He is going to Kangaroo's party.
He counts his shoes as he puts them on.
"One, two, three, four, five, six, seven..." Only seven shoes for EIGHT feet!
"Oh dear, I have lost one of my shoes," says Spider.
He looks in his house but he cannot find the shoe anywhere.

Spider goes to look for the shoe. He meets Elephant. Elephant is busy picking oranges.

"Hello, Elephant. Have you seen my shoe?" asks Spider.

"No," says Elephant, "and I am far too busy to look for it. If you see Alligator, tell him I will bring oranges to Kangaroo's party."

"I shall probably forget," says Spider.

Spider sets off to look for Alligator. As he runs along, one shiny shoe falls off. Spider does not see it. Alligator is on the muddy river bank.

"Hello, Spider," shouts Alligator. He waves his tail. SPLOSH! The mud splashes Spider's shiny shoes.

Spider forgets all about the oranges. "Look at my shoes!" he cries. "They are not shiny now."

"Sorry, Spider," says Alligator.

Spider counts his shoes. "One, two, three, four, five, six..."

"You have lost two shoes," says Alligator.

"Have you seen them?" asks Spider.

"No," says Alligator.

"Go and ask Mouse," says Alligator, "and tell her I will bring a cake to Kangaroo's party."

"I shall probably forget," says Spider. He sets off to look for Mouse. As he runs along, another shoe falls off. But Spider does not see it.

Boom! Boom! Boom!
It is Mouse. She is playing
her drum. What a noise!
"Hey, Spider!" says Mouse.
"Where are your shoes?"
Spider forgets all about
the cake. He counts his
shoes again.
"One, two, three, four,
five." Only five shoes for
EIGHT feet!

"I have lost three shoes now," says Spider. "Do you know where they are?"

"No," says Mouse. "Have you asked Lion? Maybe he can help. If you see Lion, tell him I will take my drum to Kangaroo's party."

"I shall probably forget," says Spider.

Spider sets off again.
As he runs, another shoe
falls off. He does not see it.
There is Lion. He is asleep,
as usual, under a tree.
Lion opens one eye.
"Hello, Spider. You have
lost four of your shoes,"
he says.

Spider forgets about the drum.

"Oh, not another shoe," cries Spider. He counts his shoes.

"One, two, three, four..." Four shoes for EIGHT feet! Lion is much too tired to help Spider look for them.

"Ask Kangaroo," says Lion with a yawn. "She may know."

"Oh, Spider," says Lion, "tell Kangaroo I shall bring flowers to her party." "I shall probably forget," says Spider. As he runs off, another shoe falls off. But still he does not see! He meets Kangaroo. "Hello, Spider. Where are your shoes?" she cries.

Spider forgets about the flowers. He counts his shoes.
"One, two, three..."
Only three shoes left.
Spider begins to cry.
"Cheer up, Spider," says Kangaroo. "You are just in time for my party."
"Party?" sobs Spider. "Oh dear, I forgot about your party."

Look. Here come Spider's friends. Elephant is carrying some oranges and one of Spider's shoes. Alligator has a cake and another shoe. Mouse is carrying her drum and another shoe. Lion has some flowers and another shoe. Spider begins to count.

"I have three shoes. That makes four... five... six... seven."

Poor Spider. Still only seven shoes for eight feet. But Kangaroo says, "Hey Spider. Look in my pouch. There is the lost shoe! Remember! You gave it to me yesterday to clean it," says Kangaroo. "Bring me the other seven tomorrow and I will clean them too." "Thank you," says Spider, "but I shall probably forget."

Here are some words in the story.

counts	muddy
lost	another
busy	asleep
party	opens
forget	tired
shiny	yawn
falls	pouch

What can you see?

shoes

oranges

cake

drum

flowers

The Shy Ostrich

The animals are playing bat and ball. The bat is a branch. the ball is a coconut. Elephant likes to bat. All the animals enjoy playing. All except Ostrich.

"Come on, Ostrich, join in the game," calls Kangaroo.

But Ostrich goes red and puts her bucket over her head. She is too shy to join in.

Ostrich wanders off by herself. Soon she bumps into the trees in Elephant's orange grove. She hears a noise and takes her bucket off her head. She sees Monkey taking Elephant's oranges. Ostrich wants to stop him but she is too shy. "What shall I do?" she whispers to herself. Then she thinks of something.

Ostrich puts her head in her bucket and makes a loud noise.

"Oooeraaah!" she booms. It sounds just like Elephant.

"Elephant is coming!" cries Monkey. He drops the oranges and scampers off. Ostrich picks up the oranges.

"Put them down!" says a big voice. Elephant has come back.

Ostrich tries to explain.
"I... I... Oh dear." She is too
shy. She puts her bucket
over her head and runs
off.
Elephant picks up his
oranges.
"Stupid bird," he says.
Ostrich keeps running until
she reaches Spider's
house. She hears Monkey
again. He is filling Spider's
shoes with stones.

"What shall I do?" whispers Ostrich to herself. Then she thinks of something. She finds a stick and picks up her bucket. She taps on her bucket with the stick. Faster and faster she taps. It sounds like Spider. "Spider is coming!" yells Monkey. He drops the shoes and runs away.

Ostrich starts to empty Spider's shoes. Just then Spider arrives home.

"Hey, Ostrich, what are you doing with my shoes?" he asks.

Poor Ostrich tries to explain.

"I... I... Oh dear." She is too shy. She puts her bucket over her head and runs away.

"Funny bird," says Spider.

Ostrich slows down as she reaches Kangaroo's home. She takes the bucket off. She sees Monkey again. He is messing up Baby Kangaroo's toys.

"What shall I do?" whispers Ostrich. Then she thinks of something.

She picks up a berry and she draws two eyes and a nose on her bucket. She puts vines on top for the hair. She finds a chalky stone and draws a big, scary mouth. She puts the bucket on her head and stands up in the long grass.

"Whoo! Whoo! WHOO!" shouts Ostrich.
Monkey looks up. He sees a scary face in the long grass.
"HELP! A MONSTER!" he screams. He drops the toys and runs for his life.
Ostrich takes off her bucket and begins to pick up all the toys. Then she hears a noise.

Someone is coming along the path. It is Kangaroo. "Oh, Ostrich," she says. "What are you doing with Baby's toys?"

"I... I... Oh dear." Ostrich is too shy to explain. She hides her head in her bucket and runs off. Kangaroo picks up the toys.

"Strange bird," she says.

Ostrich sits down and begins to cry into her bucket.

"I... I... I never took Elephant's oranges. I never put stones in Spider's shoes. I never played with Baby Kangaroo's toys."

"I know, I know," says a voice. It is Parrot. "I saw it all. I saw it all. It was Monkey. It was Monkey."

"I told everyone. I told everyone," says Parrot. Here they all come now. Monkey is with them. He looks very sad. "He tried to tickle Lion while he was asleep," explains Mouse. "If you promise to be a good monkey, we will let you go," says Kangaroo. "I promise," says Monkey and he runs away.

"We must have a party for Ostrich," says Kangaroo. "She is such a clever bird." So they have a party. They all sing and dance. Everyone joins in the fun. All except Ostrich. She sits in a corner with her head in a bucket. She is so shy.

Here are some words in the story.

join	booms
game	scampers
grove	stick
hears	yells
noise	scary
taking	monster
whispers	clever

What can you see?

branch

coconut

stones

vines

toys

The Clumsy Alligator

Alligator has big feet. He has a big tail too. Sometimes he trips over his big feet. Sometimes he trips over his big tail. And sometimes he trips over everything. Then all his friends laugh. They call him the Clumsy Alligator.

One day Alligator is walking along when he sees Ostrich picking plums. "Hello Ostrich," he shouts. But Alligator does not see the log Ostrich is standing on. He bumps into it. CRASH! Ostrich tumbles to the ground. The bucket lands on her head. "Oops," says Alligator.

Alligator takes the bucket off Ostrich's head. "Stay away from me, Alligator," she cries. She gets up and runs over the stepping stones to the other side of the river. "Sorry, Ostrich," shouts Alligator.

He turns away and goes to look for his friend Lion. He sees him lying in the grass. Lion is asleep as usual. Alligator runs up to his friend. But he does not see his tail. He steps on it very hard.

"Aaaarr!" roars Lion.

"Oops," says Alligator.
Lion is angry.
"You clumsy animal," says
Lion. "I am going over the
river to find a quiet place
to rest."
Lion goes across the
stepping stones.
"Sorry, Lion," says Alligator.
"Stay away from me!"
roars Lion.

Alligator heads back to his muddy bank. His friend Spider comes to see him. "Hey, Alligator," calls Spider. "Look at my new shoes!"
Alligator waves his long tail. Bits of mud go flying through the air.

Spider starts to run but it is too late. SPLASH! Down comes the mud, all over Spider's new shoes. "Oops," says Alligator. "Look at my new shoes," moans Spider. He runs away from Alligator. He goes across the river on the stepping stones.

"Sorry, Spider," shouts Alligator.
"Stay away from me," cries Spider.
Alligator decides to go and see his friend Kangaroo. She is picking flowers with her baby and Hippo.
"Hello," calls Alligator. He does not see the flowers by the path.

"Watch out!" cries Hippo, but it is too late. Alligator crushes all the flowers. "Oops," says Alligator. Baby Kangaroo starts to cry. Kangaroo picks him up and puts him in her pouch.

"Come on, Hippo," says Kangaroo. "We shall go over the river on the stepping stones."

"Sorry, everyone," shouts Alligator.

"Stay away from us," calls Hippo.

Poor Alligator. He sits down beside the crushed flowers. He feels sad.

"No one likes me because I spoil everything," he says. "I wish my feet and tail were not so big and clumsy."

The sun goes in and it gets very cold. The wind begins to blow and the raindrops start to fall. It rains and rains. Soon the river is full. Alligator can hardly see the stepping stones at all.

He sees his friends on the other side. He runs down to the river.

"Help! We cannot get back," they all cry.

"I can help," says Alligator. He steps into the river. He digs two big feet into one bank, and two big feet into the other.

"Jump on," he calls to his friends.

One by one the animals step onto Alligator's tail and walk across his back to the other side of the river.

"Three cheers for Alligator," says Kangaroo when all the animals are safely across. "We are very pleased to have a friend with such big feet and such a big tail."

Alligator smiles a very big smile.

Here are some words in the story.

trips	mud
clumsy	flowers
picking	crushes
plums	digs
tail	bank
quiet	jump
waves	smile